What's Michael?

A Hard Day's Life

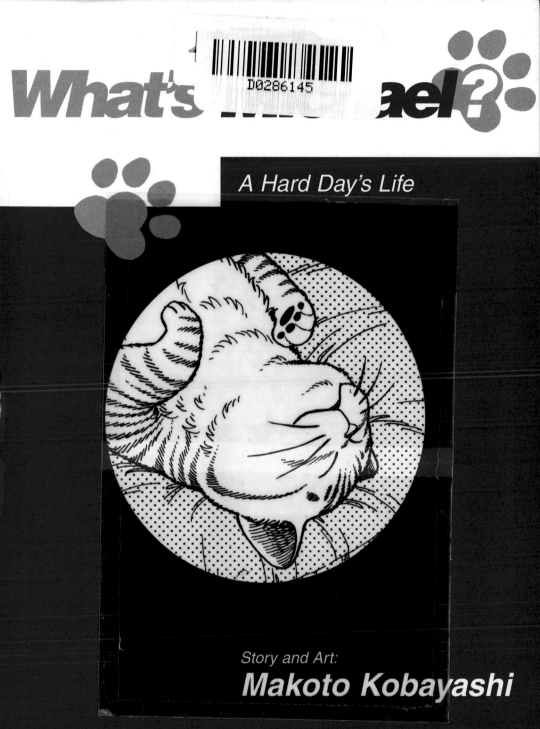

Story and Art:
Makoto Kobayashi

Translation:
Dana Lewis & **Lea Hernandez**

Dark Horse Comics, Inc.®

Lettering and Retouch:
Amador Cisneros

publisher
Mike Richardson

series editor
Mike Hansen

series executive editor
Toren Smith for **Studio Proteus**

collection editor
Chris Warner

designer and art director
Mark Cox

English-language version produced by
Studio Proteus, Radio Comix,
and **Dark Horse Comics, Inc.**

What's Michael? Vol. VI: A Hard Day's Life

This volume collects What's Michael? stories
from issues eight through fifteen of the Dark
Horse comic-book series Super Manga Blast!

The artwork of this volume has been produced
as a mirror-image of the original Japanese
edition to conform to English-language standards.

Published by
Dark Horse Comics, Inc.
10956 SE Main Street
Milwaukie, OR 97222

www.darkhorse.com

To find a comics shop in your area, call the
Comic Shop Locator Service toll-free at
1-888-266-4226

First edition: July 2002
ISBN: 1-56971-744-3

10 9 8 7 6 5 4 3 2 1

Printed in Canada

THE MOURNING FAREWELL

4

6

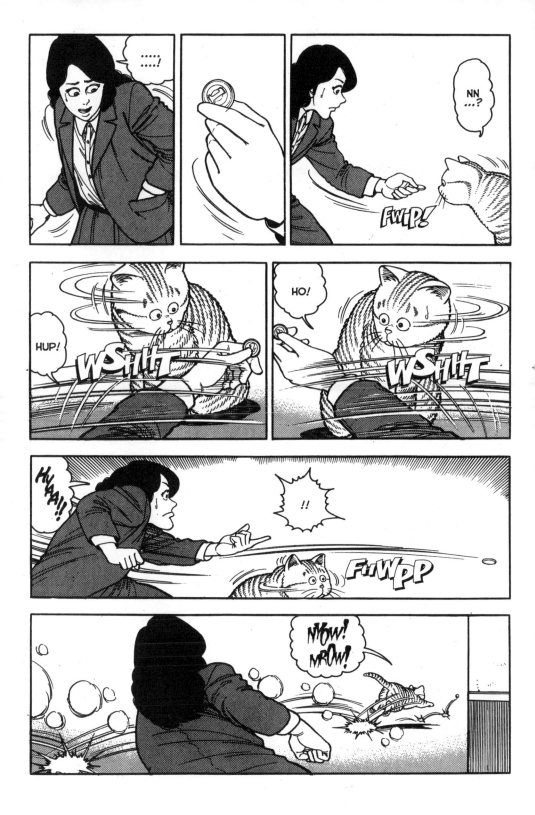

THE END

THE GUESTS WHO
WOULDN'T LEAVE:
THE HORROR CONTINUES

TIK... TIK...

TIK...

TIK...

Slp

THE GUESTS
WHO COULDN'T
CARRY A
CONVERSATION
ARE STILL
LINGERING...

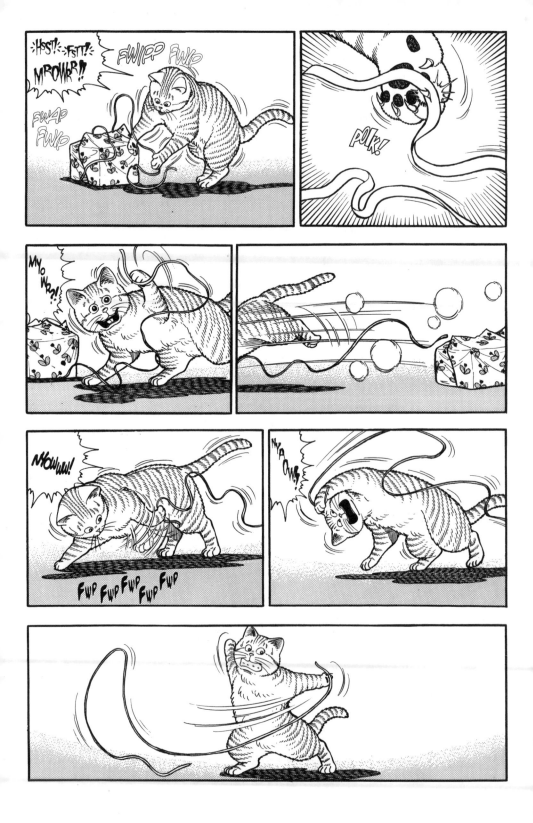

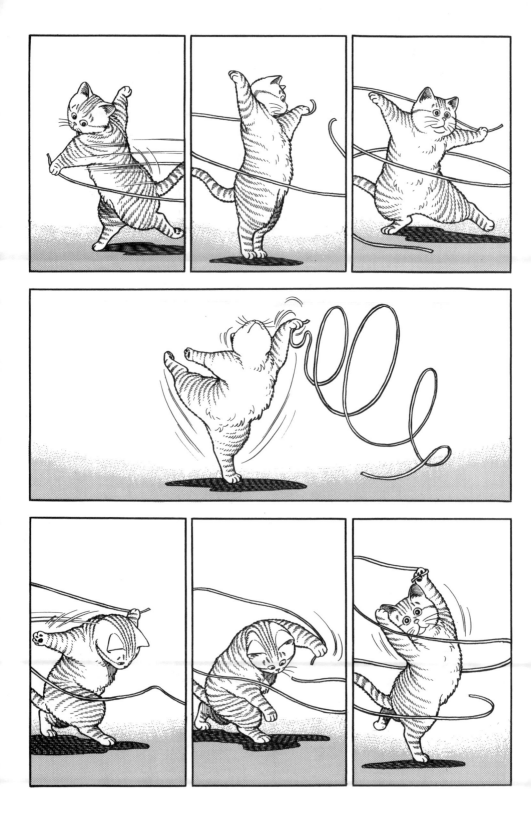

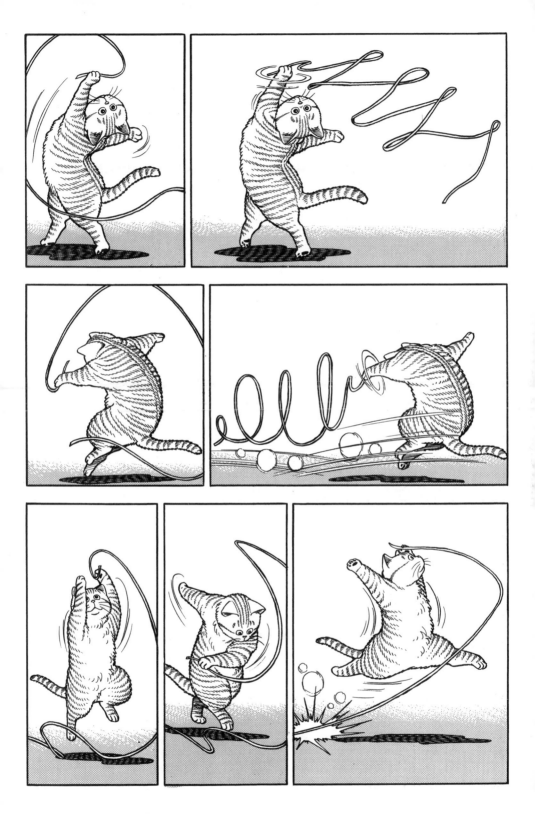

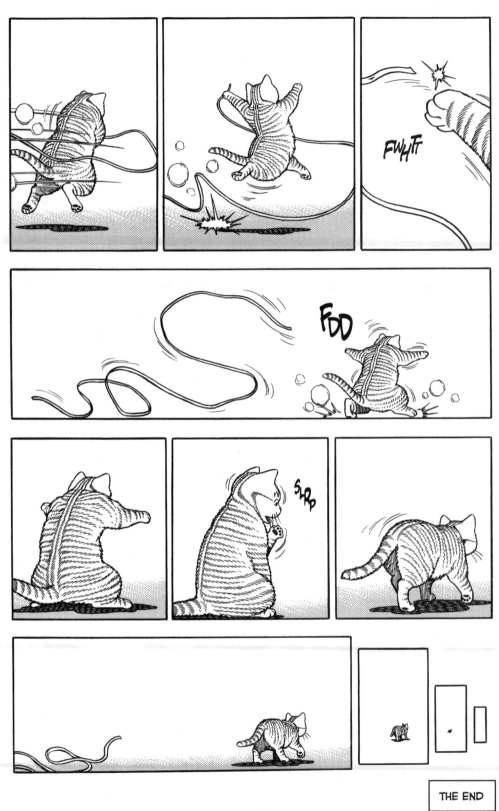

THE END

21

23

25

ANOTHER BITTER END...

30

31

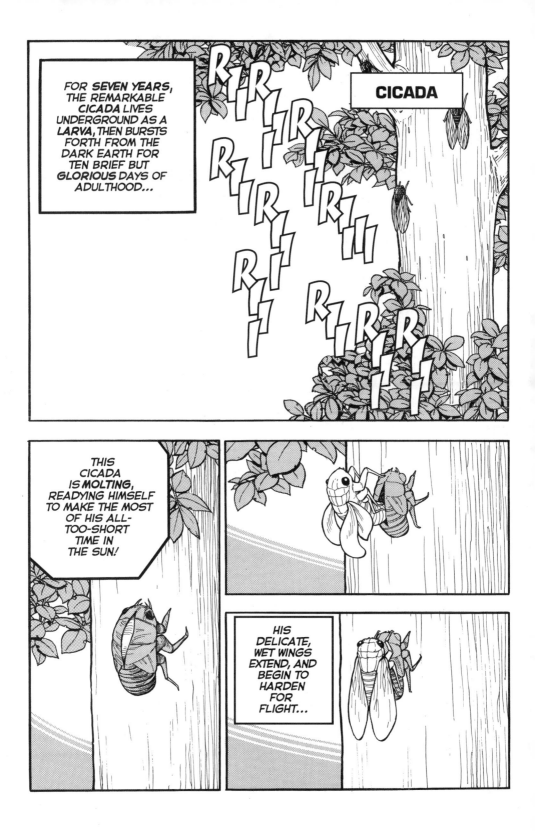

FOR **SEVEN YEARS,** THE REMARKABLE **CICADA** LIVES UNDERGROUND AS A **LARVA,** THEN BURSTS FORTH FROM THE DARK EARTH FOR TEN BRIEF BUT **GLORIOUS** DAYS OF ADULTHOOD...

CICADA

THIS CICADA IS **MOLTING,** READYING HIMSELF TO MAKE THE MOST OF HIS ALL-TOO-SHORT TIME IN THE SUN!

HIS DELICATE, WET WINGS EXTEND, AND BEGIN TO HARDEN FOR FLIGHT...

33

37

THE END

40

THE END

CAP'N BEAR'S TREASURE

45

47

48

49

THE BITTERSWEET END

THE END

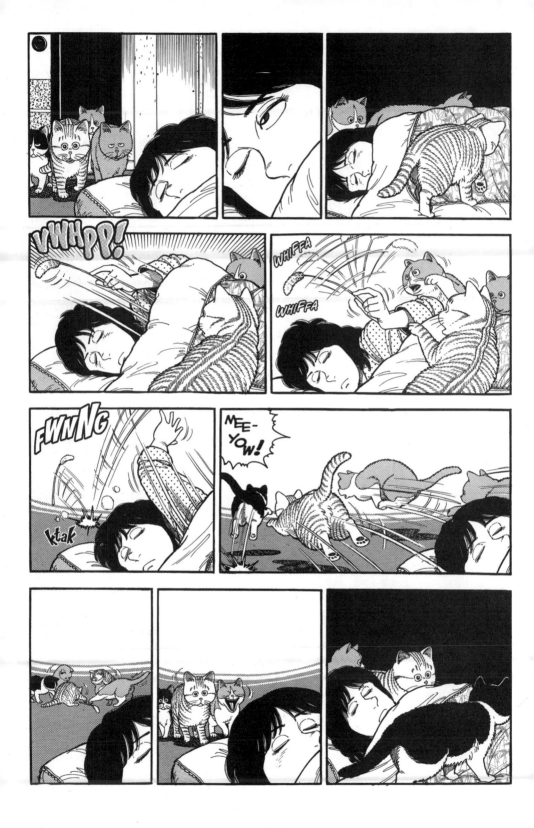

THE END

A HARD
DAY'S LIFE

THE END

NAME: *RICHARD KIMBLY.*

OCCUPATION: *VETERINARIAN*

THE FUGITIVE II

SENTENCED TO *DEATH* FOR THE MURDER OF HIS *WIFE*...AND FOR *CAT-WRAPPING*--CRIMES HE DID *NOT COMMIT!*

EN ROUTE TO *DEATH ROW,* THE DOCTOR WAS FREED BY A CHANCE *TRAIN WRECK!*

NOW HE LIVES ON THE RUN-- CONSTANTLY CHANGING HIS NAME, HIS JOB, HIS *DEODORANT!*

THE RELENTLESS *LT. GERARDLY* ALWAYS MERE MOMENTS BEHIND HIM!

AND SO... RICHARD KIMBLY'S LIFE OF DESPERATION *CONTINUES!*

76

TALES OF THE SNOW COUNTRY

TO BRAVE SOULS WHO LIVE IN THE DEEP NORTH...

...SNOW IS NOT "BEAUTIFUL," OR FOR RECREATION. SNOW IS JUST *WORK*.

OUR TALE IS OF ONE SUCH MAN, A COURAGEOUS SURVIVOR IN THIS LAND OF ICE AND SNOW!

SKSH

SKSSH

SKSH

Lady Kobayashi, *Female*

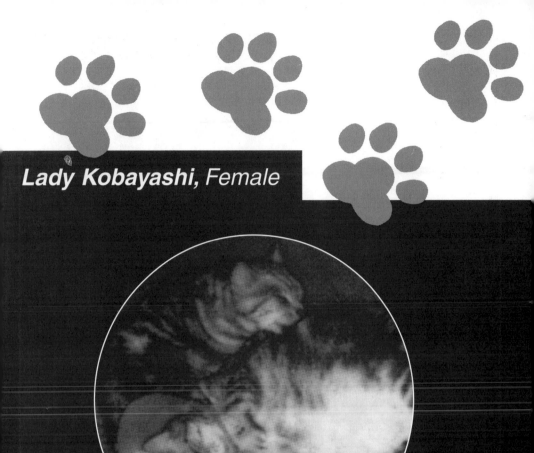

No, this isn't some drunk raccoon sleeping it off. This is Lady, Hogan's wife, and the model for Michael's wife, Popo.

Right now she's carrying a bit of weight, but when she was young she was one beautiful cat. She's a prideful creature indeed, refuses to toady to humans, and is all-around the most catlike of all our cats. But since — Did I mention this already? — she has put on a little weight, I'm always surprised when I see her

looking like this (even though I see her every day).

I know it wasn't polite to laugh, Lady, but when our eyes met, I just couldn't help myself. Sorry! You know, it's okay to ask for attention now and then. Even when you're not cold and hungry, my Lady.

— Makoto Kobayashi